D0506663

Daniel's New Friend

Adapted by Becky Friedman
Based on the screenplay written by Becky Friedman
Poses and layouts by Jason Fruchter

Simon Spotlight
New York   London   Toronto   Sydney   New Delhi

SIMON SPOTLIGHT
An imprint of Simon & Schuster Children's Publishing Division
1230 Avenue of the Americas, New York, New York 10020
This Simon Spotlight paperback edition May 2015
© 2015 The Fred Rogers Company
For information about special discounts for bulk purchases, please contact Simon & Schuster
Special Sales at 1-866-506-1949 or business@simonandschuster.com.
Manufactured in the United States of America 0915 LAK
10 9 8 7 6 5 4 3 2
ISBN 978-1-4814-3543-7
ISBN 978-1-4814-3544-4 (eBook)

It was a beautiful day in the neighborhood, and Daniel and Miss Elaina went to Prince Wednesday's castle to play.
"A royal welcome," said Queen Sara Saturday.

When Miss Elaina and Daniel got to Prince Wednesday's room, they saw someone they didn't know.

"Hi, what's your name?" asked Miss Elaina.

"That's my cousin, Chrissie," said Prince Wednesday.

"Hi, Chrissie," said Daniel.

"It's nice to know you!" Chrissie smiled.

"We're playing knights!" said Prince Wednesday.

"I'll be the big knight!" said Miss Elaina, picking a knight up from the table.

"I'll be the silver knight!" said Daniel.

"And I'll be the flying knight!" said Chrissie, making her knight fly into the air. "Look out beloooooow!"

"I want my knight to fly too!" cheered Miss Elaina.
"Me too!" said Prince Wednesday.
"Me three!" added Daniel.

Daniel, Miss Elaina, and Prince Wednesday all made their knights fly in the air, just like Chrissie.

"Whee!" the friends said, giggling as they played.

"Now let's dress up as knights!" said Prince Wednesday, "I have knight costumes."

"Grr-ific idea!" said Daniel.

Prince Wednesday asked his mom, Queen Sara Saturday, to help him find his knight costumes.

"Here they are!" Prince Wednesday exclaimed after he found the costumes in his dress-up trunk.

Daniel and Miss Elaina jumped up and ran over to Prince Wednesday to get a costume. But Chrissie didn't get up.

"Chrissie," called Daniel, "don't you want to play?"

"I'm coming," said Chrissie, "but I need my crutches to stand."
Queen Sara Saturday gave Chrissie her crutches, and Chrissie
slowly stood up. Daniel could see she had something on her legs.

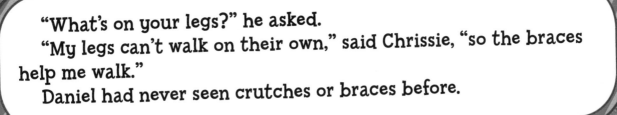

"What's on your legs?" he asked.

"My legs can't walk on their own," said Chrissie, "so the braces help me walk."

Daniel had never seen crutches or braces before.

"Can I touch your braces?" asked Daniel
"Sure!" said Chrissie. "It won't hurt me!"
Daniel felt Chrissie's braces. They felt smooth and cool.
"Do you wear your braces all the time?" asked Miss Elaina.

"Not *all* of the time," replied Chrissie. "Not when I sleep, or take a bath. But most of the time . . . I even wear them to school!"

"You go to school?" asked Daniel. "We go to school too!"

"I'm just like you," said Chrissie, "but the way I walk is different."

"In some ways we are different, but in so many ways, we are the same," said Queen Sara Saturday. "You walk differently from each other, but you are the same in other ways. You all go to school, and you all like to play. We all have things about us that are the same, and things that are different."

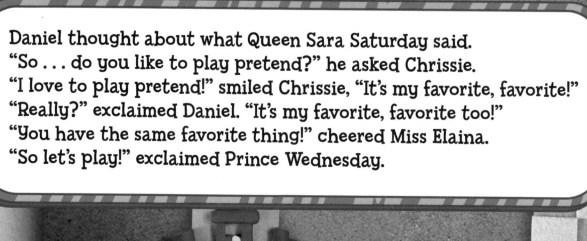

Daniel thought about what Queen Sara Saturday said.
"So . . . do you like to play pretend?" he asked Chrissie.
"I love to play pretend!" smiled Chrissie, "It's my favorite, favorite!"
"Really?" exclaimed Daniel. "It's my favorite, favorite too!"
"You have the same favorite thing!" cheered Miss Elaina.
"So let's play!" exclaimed Prince Wednesday.

"*Roar!*" said Prince Wednesday, "I'm a dragon!"
"Careful! Don't bump Chrissie!" said Daniel.
"It's okay, Daniel. Sometimes I do need extra help," said Chrissie.
"But I also like to do things by myself . . . just like you! And right now I'm Brave Knight Chrissie!"

"Come on, knights!" said Miss Elaina. "Let's stop that dragon!" Daniel, Prince Wednesday, and Miss Elaina ran around Prince Wednesday's room. Around and around they went, until Daniel noticed . . . Chrissie was going slower than everyone else.

"Come on Knight Chrissie!" exclaimed Daniel. "We have to go fast to catch the dragon!"

But Chrissie shook her head. "I can't go as fast as you can," she explained.

"Oh no," said Daniel, "if you can't go as fast as us, then maybe we should stop playing!"

But Chrissie didn't want to stop playing. "I like being a knight!" she told Daniel. "I just need to play a different way."

"What do you mean?" asked Daniel.

"When you play knight, you run around. When I play knight, I stand, and guard the castle!" Chrissie explained.

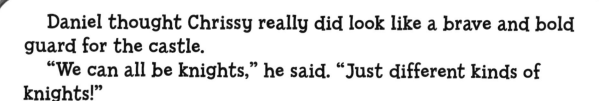

Daniel thought Chrissy really did look like a brave and bold guard for the castle.

"We can all be knights," he said. "Just different kinds of knights!"

"Not me!" said Prince Wednesday. "I'm different. Because I'm a dragon!"

"Come on, knights!" said Daniel. "Let's stop that dragon!"